THE HIKE TO HIGHER GROUND

Also by Alyssa Feliciano

Love's Flame: A Romantasy Short Story

THE HIKE TO HIGHER GROUND

A NOVELLA

Alyssa Feliciano

attic

an imprint of Nicole Frail Books, LLC
Avoca, Pennsylvania

To my husband Chris,
Thank you for supporting me in all my
dreams, hobbies, and passions.

This one's for you.

Prologue

LEAH

AT 6:56, I PULL MY phone out of my purse for the first time all day. Today was brutal; my schedule was so packed with client meetings and court appearances that I didn't even pause for lunch. My stomach grumbles at the mere thought of food.

I notice a text from Grayson, my fiancé. "Long day. Working late. Don't wait up."

Oh, that's convenient! I decide I'll order us Thai from our favorite place and surprise him with dinner in his office, which is just down the other hallway past the elevators. Living in the city that never sleeps means having hundreds of food options at my fingertips. With a few clicks, the order is in.

I make my way down the hall to the elevator and ride to the ground level to await the Uber Eats delivery. I take a seat in the lobby on one of the lounge chairs and relax for the first time since I opened my eyes at five this morning. I hear my phone ding and sneak a peek to find a text from my mother. I decide to just call her.

She answers on the first ring.

"Hi, Mom."

"Hi, sweetie. Are you working late again?" she asks, concerned.

"You know it. Grayson is here late, too, so I just ordered us some dinner."

"You need to take care of yourself. Your father and I miss you. When can you make a trip home?"

She's been asking me to visit them for the past six months.

"I am *really* busy here, Mom. If I want to get this next promotion, I need to keep up. I promise before the holidays that we'll come. Oh—I have to go. My food's here. Love you, bye."

I hang up before she barely gets out the word *goodbye*.

The food is not here, but I needed to avoid the conversation about coming home. It'll just make both of us upset. I never feel like I have time to go home.

I sigh and sit back in the chair to commence scrolling through Instagram. My feed these days has been filled with beautiful reels of the best views from people who are hiking all these amazing places. I can feel my heart crack a bit. The only "hiking" I have done lately has been around Central Park.

I roll my eyes, shut off the screen, and place my phone in my pocket. This job does keep me from a lot of the things I love, including my family. Saddened at the thought that I haven't traveled or even done any *real* hiking lately, I throw my head back and sink further into the chair, closing my eyes for a moment.

When I open them, I'm staring at the sign for our law firm: P&S Law. It's the top firm in the city. Grayson and I both got hired right out of NYU, which honestly seems so much longer than three years ago. We are both coming up on promotions this year, so we have both been deep in client relations and attempting to make our names stand out and *matter*.

A quick rap on the front door pulls me from my thoughts. Ah, my food!

My smile must be contagious, because the gentleman holding my food can't help but return the sentiment. I open the door, practically drooling at the immediate smell of the green curry and pad thai.

"Thank you!" I exclaim, reaching for the bag.

"You're welcome. Have a good night," the man replies, handing me two bags.

I look down, confused, and I quickly yell out the door to stop the man.

"Excuse me, sir! I only placed one order. I think you may have made a mistake." I gesture to the second bag.

"Oh, I'm sorry. I assumed you were picking up the order for Leah, as well. I'm sorry for the mix up. I will send a notification for that order and wait here." He reaches out to retrieve *my* order.

But now I'm even more confused. I look down at the names on the receipts stapled to the bags and I see my name, Leah, on the front of one. And across the second bag is an order for Grayson.

"Miss?" the man questions, breaking the awkward silence.

"I'm sorry. I *am* Leah, this one order is mine, and it looks like the other order is actually for my fiancé, Grayson. We both work for P&S. I was trying to surprise him with dinner, but I guess he already ordered for himself. I'll take it up to him." I smile at the patient man.

I reach into my pocket and hand him an extra five-dollar tip for his delay.

"Okay, yeah, he sure must work hard. That's the third time this week I dropped off food for him so late." He smiles, takes the five dollars from me, and then strides off, assuming back to his bike.

The third time this week? I heft the bag up to eye level, and the sheer size and weight of it alone tells me there's a good amount of food inside. *Definitely more than one person usually eats.* I try to shrug off the negative voice in my head and return to the elevator. Grayson has never given me reason to distrust him.

A small pit forms in my stomach anyway.

I ride the elevator back up to the top floor of the building, and instead of going left toward my office, I go right to make my way to Grayson's. Despite my uneasiness, I'm still looking forward to seeing him. It's been such a long day.

But as I get closer, I hear what sounds like a groan coming from the direction of Grayson's office. I slowly round the corner and immediately stop dead in my tracks. It takes far too long for my mind to catch up to the sight before me.

I am utterly frozen in place. My legs are blocks of lead that I can't seem to move. My eyes are burning, unblinking.

Grayson is at his desk, lips locked with someone sitting on top of his desk, her legs wrapped around his waist.

The Thai food scatters across the hallway floor, right alongside shards of my heart. I don't even remember the bags slipping from my hand, but my fists are now empty.

Grayson must have heard the food containers hit the floor, because he abruptly stops mid-kiss, and his eyes flit over her shoulder to investigate.

But what he finds is *me* staring back at him.

His face drains of every color. Even the usually charming vibrance of his blue eyes seems to dissipate.

"Grayson! Hello? What is it?" The sultry woman's voice travels through the silent office space, thawing my frozen state as she runs a hand up his large, muscular arm and tries to pull his attention back to her.

She flips her long, blonde hair and peeks over her shoulder to lock eyes with me. She doesn't flinch, just smirks devilishly. I immediately recognize her as Jolene Providence, the "P" in P&S Law firm. My mouth drops open as Grayson backs away from her and tries to compose himself.

He starts pulling away from the intimate embrace he was in with Jolene. "Leah, it's not—"

"What?! It's not exactly what it looks like?" I hammer at him, pointing beside him.

I can feel the tears welling up, lodging in my throat. *I will not cry.*

I turn, hot on my heels, and charge back toward my own office, leaving Grayson and the whole mess without a second thought.

I lock my office door behind me and gather my things quickly. I pick up the lone photograph of Grayson and me at our engagement photoshoot and debate hurling it at the wall. *No, I won't give him that satisfaction. Slow to anger, Leah.*

Despite the burning rage beginning to set a course through me, I grab my laptop and stuff my favorite paperweight into my purse. I can hear Grayson outside the door, begging me to open it.

"Leah, let me explain!" He attempts the door handle as he implores me to open it.

I march toward the door, fling it open, and stride right past Grayson, dropping my engagement ring to the floor beside him as I go.

Without a word, I leave and don't look back. *I don't deserve this.*

I haul out of that building faster than I ever have in three years. I hail a taxi and give them my parents' address. The twenty-five-minute drive won't even be enough to process everything before I get there. Once I am in the confines of the taxi and we pull away from the curb and into New York City traffic, the tears start. And they flow like a faucet I can't turn off.

I send one text to my mother. The one she's been waiting for, though admittedly under different circumstances.

Me: I'm coming home.

Then I turn my phone settings to silent; Grayson has already tried calling me.

The next thing I do is call my best friend, Chelsea.

"Hey, girl. Late night?" Chelsea's happy tone floods my ears.

I say nothing for a beat as I try not to choke on my

tears. But who am I kidding? This is my best friend. She knew within that single moment of silence that something was wrong.

"Is this one of those times where I need to don a disguise and ask no questions? Cause my inflatable unicorn costume from 2014 Halloween is handy." She's playful but serious, which helps me not sob, but I know she can hear the sniffle beyond my small laugh.

When I am sure the words will come out coherent, I calmly ask her, "Can you meet me at my parents?"

"On my way," Chelsea says, and I can already hear her rummaging through her house, searching for her purse and keys.

Chapter 1

LEAH

Three Months Later

NOBODY WARNS YOU ABOUT HOW change is not only inevitable, but how it can quite literally hit you like a Mack truck.

I, Leah, like order and organization in all aspects of my life. I knew from a young age where I wanted to go to college and what I wanted to be, and I had a very specific vision of what marriage would look like and when it would happen. I made every one of my aspirations a reality. I worked hard to become someone my parents would be proud of. I graduated from NYU Law School with honors, got a job at my first-choice firm, and I had a boyfriend who would work alongside me and became my fiancé. I was ecstatic a year ago when Grayson had asked me to marry him. Life was exactly what I had envisioned for myself.

And then that Mack truck came along three months ago. And all those aspirations, all those boxes I seemed to have checked off, imploded. And it crushed me.

The day after I found Grayson cheating on me, I called and quit the firm and put my townhouse up for sale. I officially signed the townhouse over a week ago and gathered the last of my things that I didn't leave for the buyer. I've put most of the furniture that I wanted to keep in a storage unit until I figure out where I am headed next.

I've tried to hold my head high despite the overwhelming feeling of failure that still clings to me. Although, I do have to admit there is something liberating about the entire scenario. It feels like I've shed a weight I hadn't known I'd been carrying.

"This is the last one from the basement, sweetie." My mother's voice breaks my thoughts as she places a box inside my new-slash-old room. "You doing okay?"

"Thank you. Yes, I'll be okay. Each day gets easier. Just feeling disappointed."

"Disappointed over what exactly?" She hands me the box she'd brought in.

I place the box on my bed and turn to look at her.

"I'm a twenty-eight-year-old who just quit her job, moved back in with her parents, and broke off her engagement. I should be moving forward not backward," I tell her, exasperated.

"I see. Well, you're not disappointing anyone. Sometimes how we think life should be and how it needs to be are two very different paths. God has a plan, dear. And for what it's worth, we love having you home."

She plants a soft kiss on my head and leaves the room.

Maybe *disappointed* is the wrong word. I think I feel shame.

My parents' house has always been the same, which is comforting. I grew up in this house, this town. Roan, New Jersey, has always been my home, but I miss its smallness, what it was before it was commercialized and became a tourist attraction. Now, it's an American Dream Mall area and booming with franchised businesses. I don't know what my next step will be, but I don't think staying in Roan for too long is part of it.

My phone rings, and I glance over at the name *Chelsea* displayed on the screen. I grab it without hesitation.

"Hey."

"Hi Lee. I am coming over and hanging out with you for a bit," my best friend states.

Chelsea and I have been friends since kindergarten, and right now she's the only semblance of my life that is still the same. When I came back home three months ago, she was here waiting for me that night. I cried in her arms for hours and she didn't ask any questions. She just was there.

The next day, I told her the whole story, and she'd replied, "So where should we hide the body?"

I check the clock to confirm the time. "Of course. When will you be here? I'll get us lunch."

"I'm already here and got us subs," Chelsea says, and I know she's smiling at herself. I can tell by her amused tone.

"You know the way to my heart. Doors open." I hang up and smile, shaking my head at how well she knows me.

I walk over to the box my mom brought up and open it. This box is my travel box: a mix of reminders of all the places I had hoped to travel among other trinkets I collected from the places that I did make it to, mostly before I started my job. I lift the box and dump it across my bedspread. *Easier to see it all*, I reason.

Chelsea enters my room and extends a wrapped piece of heaven toward me. "Hey girl, I got you the Italian sub, extra oil and vinegar, *no* veggies."

"You know I love you!" I tell her, reaching for it.

She stands at my side and begins rummaging through all the things I'd just dumped across my bed.

"What's all this?" she asks.

"Oh, just trinkets from the traveling I had done or small keepsakes," I tell her.

She picks up a framed photo of me and three other girls covered in splashes of color and showing off gold medals from a Color Run 5k I had done.

"Ah, I remember this! It looked so fun! I was sorry to have missed it. Have you spoken to any of these girls since?" she asks me, staring at the photo with a smile.

"I haven't spoken to them in close to three years. This was right before Grayson and I got hired at the firm. It was one of the last true runs I did. Grayson never liked hiking or running, just the gym and beaches, so time became limited for outdoor activities," I tell her and then reach for the photo and examine the girls one by one. "Sarah went on to run 5k's around the world. The other two, Mira and Bianca, settled down and had kids. We grew apart." I can hear the sorrow in my tone.

"You know you made the right choice leaving him, don't you?" Chelsea doesn't intend for me to answer her question. "I mean, you literally gave up your love of outdoor adventure, which meant giving up a lot of your friendships and general happiness. For him. What did he give up for you?"

I know she's right, but I still feel the sting of her words.

Chelsea notes the silence and changes the subject.

"I don't remember you going to Moab?" she asks,

picking up a brochure of Arches National Park and looking intently at it.

"I didn't do that one. It was my biggest dream trip and work got in the way, so I never made that one happen," I tell her.

She gives me a side glance, knowing it wasn't just work. Grayson got in the way.

I open the sub and take a bite, relishing the sweet and tangy sensation of the oil and vinegar as it hits my tongue. I close my eyes and groan in approval of this amazing sandwich.

"You should go now then! *Work* isn't a problem anymore." She stops and jumps with excitement. Her tone on the word *work* was meant to imply Grayson. *It's not missed.*

"Oh, look! Our photo from The Smokies is in here!" Chelsea says, grabbing our photo and smiling, turning to show it to me. "Look at your smile here! You need a good trip!" she adds.

I slowly sit on the edge of my bed, contemplating her words. Chelsea has an amused smile across her face. She's right, though. I am jobless at the moment, and I had signed a non-compete. So finding a new job is going to prove tricky, especially since my non-compete was very over the top. I can't work within a one-hundred-dred-mile radius of P&S. And considering my parents live within that radius, I need to look farther away. I did have a nice payout from my townhouse sale, so I don't have to rush into finding a new job. I could use this time and money to recenter myself. Live a little for me.

"Honestly, Chelsea, that's not a bad idea," I say, returning the smile and picking up the brochure she'd set aside when she found our Smokies photo.

"What's not?" My mom suddenly appears in the doorway. "Thought I heard your voice, Chelsea."

"Hi, Mrs. Peterson. Leah here never got to take that trip out west she always wanted. I told her now would be the perfect time to go," Chelsea answers.

My mother gasps at the thought. "Alone?"

I chuckle and remind her: "I am a strong, wise, independent woman."

The look she shoots makes me unsure she's entirely convinced by my statement before she leaves the room. But as I stare at the brochure, I feel this unction build up inside my spirit that pushes me to go. My father taught me a lot about hiking and camping when I was a kid, and the more I remember about the times he and I went camping, the more confident I am that I can complete a trip like this on my own.

"You said it yourself over the last few months: you feel like you need a reset. You've always loved the outdoors. Go, find peace and pray for guidance through this messy time," Chelsea tells me as she places an arm around me and squeezes just a bit.

"Why don't you come with me?" I say to her. "It

would be so fun, just the two of us!" I jump up at the thought.

"I wish beyond anything I could come with you. But I have a huge presentation at the magazine for cover ideas. This could be a big break for me. I'm sorry, I can't turn it down. And I used all but one vacation day on the trip I took to Miami a few months back," she says and shrinks back.

"No! Don't be sorry. You worked hard for cover design. I wouldn't want you to miss that opportunity. I regret not going with you to Miami." I hug her in congratulations.

"Thanks. You should still consider going," she tells me while still squeezing tightly.

I lift my head and back out of our hug. I stand, deciding that this is the start of my redemption story. What better place to find God and the reset I'm after than in the solitude of the desert where nobody and nothing can bother me?

Chapter 2

LEAH

Three Weeks Later

THE SKY IS MESMERIZING OUT here. The nights are cool, but the days are hot. *My favorite!* The stars in a cloudless sky actually seem to twinkle, confirming the vastness of their background abyss.

I lay against the cool ground of Moab, Utah, with my arms behind my head like a makeshift pillow soaking in the peace of my surroundings. Aside from the crickets and the slight crackle of my small fire, it is silent out here. *I love it.*

I had not realized how much I missed the outdoors. Never again will I let myself ignore the beauty of nature for anyone. I have always had an admiration for travel and almost anything outdoor-activity related, hiking and sightseeing being my favorite. But my hunger for climbing the career ladder had kept me in the city. And if I'm honest with myself, yes, my ex-fiancé kept me there even more.

Don't go there.

I take the thoughts of him captive and bind them up. I envision literally throwing them into a garbage can. And I say a prayer to keep all thoughts of him away. No need to taint the present day.

I yawn and decide to give in, abandoning the beauty of the summer night air for my sleeping bag in my one-person tent. It may have taken me three weeks to research everything and book the trip, but being here these last two days has been amazing! I've always wanted to go hiking and sightseeing through Moab, Utah. I have been basking in the views and sights. My camera roll is filled with tons of great photos, some of which I personally think could be published in print magazines. Maybe I'll make photography my new career. I laugh a little to myself at that. Truthfully, I love being a lawyer, but I think I need to find a better work-life balance and a place that values personal time off. I drift off, snuggled into my bag, thinking all about my most anticipated stop on my list, Arches National Park, where I will be heading in the morning.

About seven hours later, after eating a peanut butter

sandwich—a minimalist's breakfast—I closed up my tent and packed everything into my camping backpack. Ready to seize the day, I put the bag on my shoulders and hiked out of the wilderness and back to where I'd parked my car. Yesterday's hike hadn't been long; the goal for yesterday had been more about sleeping on the mountain top with the unobstructed views of the sky.

I know I'm about two hours away from my next stop. The weather is supposed to be breathtaking today, and so far it is. The sky is a bright blue with little to no clouds and it's about 75 degrees right now, though the reports said the high would be around 80. I may beg for some cloud coverage today with the hike I have planned, but the sun feels great on my skin. It feels like I'm soaking in the good and getting ready to sweat away the bad. I place my sunglasses on my face with a huge smile and start the next leg of my adventure.

Two hours later, I park my car in the designated lot and notice they have a shower/restroom area. Taking a shower and freshening up sounds like a good idea before heading out again. Roughing it is no joke. Once I feel clean enough, I head back to my car and rummage through my bag, only keeping what's necessary. I also put on my sunblock, wanting to avoid sunburn at all costs. My phone dings with a message.

Mom: You still alive out there? Send something for confirmation of life.

I smile and take a selfie of myself holding a thumbs-up and send that off in a text to her.

Me: all good here mom. I'll check in later or tomorrow not sure how service will be out here.

Mom: My gorgeous girl. Enjoy. Xo

I put my phone away and retrieve my guide map of the park. Today's hike will bring me through the first stretch of the park. I plan to camp out there and continue onto the second half of the park tomorrow. I'm a fast hiker, so I anticipate it will take me two days to get through the whole 136-mile park. But if it takes longer, so be it. I have no timeline to worry about or weigh me down.

Throughout the first three hours of my hike, I stopped multiple times to take in the immaculate views and photograph the moments. But now I'm coming up on one of the views I most awaited, The Courthouse Towers. Now is a great time to have lunch, so I take out my peanut butter and jelly sandwich and park my butt on the ground under the shadow of one of the massive towers. The giant rocks are all such a warm combination of red and orange hues. If it weren't hot outside, the ambiance alone would warm my soul. *Photos do this view no justice.*

I rest here a bit, taking deep breaths, and allow myself to come to terms with how my life feels completely upside down. With each exhale, the feeling lessens, and I remind myself that I made the right choice. I know God has a plan for my life, and right now it may not be what I thought it would look like, but I trust him. I feel peace, like waves gliding along the shoreline, come over me. On my last exhale, I stand and leave my past behind, making a promise to myself to only look forward from now on.

As I take my last bite and drink some water, I notice a slight wind beginning to pick up and the sky filling with dark-gray clouds on the northern horizon. I pause a moment to figure out which direction the clouds are moving. *Of course* they're headed in this direction. I assess where I am in the park and determine the closest location to hunker down in case it begins to rain. I check my phone's weather app only to get confirmation that rain is moving swiftly in this direction.

Twenty minutes later, I make it to a flat area and remove my tent from my bag. I take note of the clouds above, how they have now turned into a combination of gray and charcoal. *I should hurry.* The humidity in the air is making my hair stick to me and I'm a sweaty mess. I race against the clouds that are now swallowing the sun whole.

As soon as the sun is gone, the darkness cast overhead is so deep and thick that I no longer have a shadow. Lighting strikes, causing me to fumble my hands and drop one of my tent spikes. The crack of thunder that follows vibrates the ground beneath me. I relentlessly search for the tent spike, and that's when the skies open and the downpour begins.

Really? I say to nobody but myself.

I am soaked through within minutes.

"Where is that spike?!" I yell.

The rain is falling so hard and fast I can barely see my hands in front of me. Another blinding strike of lightning and a vicious crack of thunder are enough to send me scrambling for cover in my tent. *Spike be damned.*

The rain is ruthless as it pelts the tent and the outside. The roof of my tent is collecting rain because I had no time to get the rain guard up. I stand, pushing the roof up to release the puddle forming in it, when I realize the inside of my tent has become a pool around my feet. Abandoning the roof, I unzip my tent just enough to peek out and terror grips my insides. The river that was about a football field away from me is now maybe only twenty feet from me. I thought I would have been far enough away. But then again, I never guessed a monsoon would arrive on what was *supposed to be* such a beautiful day.

"The rain must be causing a flash flood. I have to move," I say to myself.

I retreat back into my tent, reaching for the map so I can figure out where to go, find the higher ground away from the river. I was a girl scout as a kid, and my dad loved camping, so he taught me everything there is to know about being out here in "God's country." I have been lucky with the weather this entire trip—*until now.*

I set a course based on the map and simultaneously decide I will have to abandon the tent because the water is quickly rising to my lower shins. I grab my phone and backpack, which, thankfully, I'd hung from a carabiner on the inside of the tent to keep it off the ground (*thanks for the tip, Tik Tok!*).

I count down aloud to bolster my courage. "Three, two, one!"

On "one," I unzip and rush out, making my way west of the tent toward the hill to higher ground. The rain slaps against my fast-moving body. I am trudging across mud, trying not to lose a shoe in the process. I'm careful to listen for cracks from the rocks in case any decide to fall. The wind has picked up more, making my hair blow into my face despite being in a high ponytail. I am about three quarters of the way up the hill, focusing really hard to not sli—

"AHH!"

A slight mudslide catches my foot and sends me careening back down the hill on my stomach. When I hit the bottom, my ego is definitely hurt, but right now the adrenaline coursing through my veins isn't allowing me to feel if anything else took any damage. The need for survival has taken over.

I rise to my feet slowly and can feel my heart pounding in my ears. I chance a look back, and the river has risen so much that my tent has been washed away. The serene, slow-moving river from mere hours ago is now looking like the Grand Rapids.

This is not good.

My anxiety is building.

"I do not want to die out here, God," I say, frantically looking around for a new plan.

I'm going to have to abandon my backpack. I shuck it off, only keeping my phone, which is in a Ziplock bag. *Thank you, Dad, for that tip.* I put that into my pocket.

The rain is barreling down, washing the mud off me. And despite it cooling me off from the earlier heat of the day, I wish it would stop.

Suddenly, I hear a crack and cannot decipher fast

enough which direction it came from. I throw my arms over my head and crouch down, hoping nothing lands on me, and then I am suddenly and forcefully shoved to the side.

A loud crash sounds in the vicinity.

Chapter 3

PIERCE

I GROAN AND REACH ACROSS my nightstand, silencing my alarm. I roll onto my back and wipe the sleep from my face as I sit up, noting the time as six o'clock. I move my legs off the bed and place my feet on the floor. I sit on the edge of my bed and take a few more minutes to wake up. My thoughts go back to last night's failed date. *I am done with Tinder.*

Rhee, I think her name was, seemed really nice through our messages, but once we were in person, I felt I got catfished. Thankfully she looked like her picture, but she had lied about her job. Maybe that seems trivial to some, but to me, with my past experiences with women, I don't do shady or lies. Turned out Rhee is an entrepreneur who makes Tik-Toks for a living, not a finance manager.

"So why does your profile say finance manager?" I asked.

"Well, I travel a lot and have to manage my expenses, so ya know, same difference, right?" she had said, twirling her blonde hair around one finger while sipping her espresso martini.

I groan at the thought again and stand up, willing the night to just go away. The kicker, though, was she had thought there would be a second date. I scoff. Dating today is not for the weary. Nobody seems to be who they say they are.

I need to not be sitting at my desk today. *A hike sounds better than work.* I check the day's weather on my phone.

No matter where I've lived, if I needed to clear my head, the outdoors always did it for me. I'd run the beach or walk the park by a lake. Since moving out here, though, I have access to national parks, which are so much more exhilarating and renewing.

I'll close the office today and head to Arches National Park for a night. I have nothing on my schedule that can't wait a few days. This is the beauty of owning my own business. I send Jane, my administrative assistant, a text.

> Me: Jane, I am taking a few personal
> days. Feel free to close early.
> I'll pay you for the trouble.

Jane: That bad last night? Okay enjoy.
I'll take phone calls and file some things
today.

Me: bad doesn't cover it.
Enjoy your days.

About an hour later, I'm all packed up for a few days of solitude, camping, and hiking. The drive over to the park was filled with refreshing and revitalizing sunshine. I park my car and step out and am immediately greeted with warm air and nothing but the smell of desert. Backpack in hand, I head into the park. *All before ten a.m.* This will work out great, because I'll get past Courthouse Towers and have lunch and reach a camping spot in great time.

The first leg of the hike is nothing but peaceful. I love watching the birds and nature simply exist around me while I walk through it. All the walking does make me hungry, though. I find a good boulder to sit against that gives me some shade from the beating sun. I packed some trail mix packs, protein bars, and a peanut butter and jelly sandwich. I'll eat my sandwich now and save the snacks for later tonight. I sit and open my ears to the world around me. Once my sandwich is gone, I don't move. I just sit there and close my eyes a bit.

I hear a distant rumbling sound that causes me to open my eyes and sit up, taking in my surroundings. Most animals wouldn't come out at peak sunshine. After a quick glance around, I look up to the sky and see black storm clouds in the far-off distance making their way this direction—and quickly. *Oh.* Time to bunker down.

I waste no time gathering my things and heading west toward the mountain. *I'll make camp on top of the hill, not too close to the edge though.* I'll be safe from the river if it flash floods.

A few miles and several minutes later, I'm racing against the clouds to set up my one-person tent. And I'm pretty sure I set it up in record time. Five minutes after I got inside, the onslaught of rain began, hammering the outside of the tent. I pull out my cell phone to check the radar, and sure enough a flash flood warning has been issued. They're calling for an immense amount of rain to fall within just thirty minutes. *Wow, that river down there will rise fast.* I say a quick and silent prayer for safety.

Feeling relatively set and safe, I can't help but sneak a peek outside my tent, and it's hard to even see a foot in front of me from the sheets of rain falling from the sky. But then I hear a noise against the crackles and thunder that sounds eerily like a person yelling. Concern draws me out of my tent and into the downpour.

I peer over the hillside, and sure enough, I see a

woman slide to the bottom. I look beyond her and realize the river has made its way well past its usual edge and is quickly pooling toward the base of this hill. I race to the edge of the hill, carefully but efficiently placing my feet so I don't also fall.

When I reach the bottom, she's maybe thirty feet away from me. She can't see me through the buckets of rain. I don't want to startle her, but I need to help her. And fast. Just as I make my move, I hear the death crackle of a boulder shifting loose, and my instinct to protect overtakes all rational thought. I run right for her.

Next thing I know, I full-on slam into her, knocking her to the ground beneath me.

I feel the boulder crash, sending vibrations through the ground.

I look up to see it landed exactly where she had been standing a moment ago.

Chapter 4
LEAH

"HEY! ARE YOU ALRIGHT? DID I hurt you?" A man's voice penetrates my ears.

I blink my eyes to focus on the sight before me. I am still lying on the ground, and my eyes widen at the fact that this burly, soaking-wet man is on top of me. I dare a peek past his shoulder and see a large boulder had crashed down right where I was standing. I make the executive decision to reflect on that later.

He peels himself from me and our clothes are so soaked through that they stick together from the contact. I get up off the ground and come to stand face to face with him. Well, more like my face to his chest, because he has to be at least five-foot-ten to my five feet. *He asked me a question,* my subconscious reminds me.

"I'm okay. Thank you!" I yell over the storm.

He nods and extends his hand to me. "Come with me! My shelter is up the hill! I'll help you up!" he shouts with urgency.

I take a beat. This is the exact thing your parents tell you not to do. But I did just tell God that I didn't want to die out here. And what other options do I have right now? And he did just save my life, I think. So, I take his hand and he more than pulls me up the hill to his campsite. All the while the rain hasn't let up. Not even for a second.

Within a few minutes, we are in the terribly small confines of his tent. Both dripping wet from the rain. He offers me a towel silently, and I hesitantly take it.

I break the silence and ask a rather dumb question. "This isn't the part where you kill me, is it?"

The man laughs. "I mean, would a murderer answer yes to that?" He quirks a brow at me, still chuckling. He then offers me a granola bar. I slowly reach to take it from him when he speaks again. "It's that or trail mix. It's all I have, sorry. My name is Pierce, by the way."

"Oh, I'm okay, but that's kind of you." I try to give it back.

"No, it's alright, really. Go ahead." He reassures me.

I open the granola bar and break it in half. "Here, please. My name is Leah," I tell him while giving him half of the snack.

He takes the bar, wrapping it into the package to save for later.

We sit in silence while I eat the granola bar. The rain still beats outside, creating some sound to ease this very awkward situation.

"Thanks for your help, by the way. This is some storm, huh?" I ask him, because I can't do awkward silence.

"Yeah, it is. Moab hasn't had a flash flood this bad in a while. But they can happen," he tells me.

"Oh, I wasn't aware it could be this bad. I must have missed that in all my research." I blush, feeling silly that I hadn't realized any of this could happen, hadn't been prepared for it.

"What brings you out here?" he asks, thankfully changing the subject, which eases my slight embarrassment.

"Just traveling and clearing my head. I always wanted to come to Moab, so I finally made that happen," I answer. "You?"

"Sightseeing, as well, I guess. I needed a break from society," he replies. "Are you sure you aren't hurt anywhere? I didn't mean to push you so hard." His tone is apologetic, sincere.

I think for a moment and then start moving parts of my body, paying closer attention as I do so. I can't help but wince when my left ankle tweaks a bit. Pierce must notice from my face.

"Where does it hurt?" he asks.

"My left ankle. I must have sprained it with the fall down the hill. Adrenaline must have kept the pain at bay until now," I tell him.

I reach for my hiking shoe and untie it. I remove my shoe and roll up my very wet, very stuck-to-my-skin pant leg. I take off my sock and reveal an angry red swollen ankle.

"Ouch," I say it out loud even though it doesn't hurt that much. Yet.

Pierce reaches into his bag and pulls out one of those instant ice packs. He crushes the package to activate the cold pack. I sit with my knees hugged to my chest, trying not to impede his space.

"Here you go, put this on." He extends me the cold pack.

"Thank you. I'm sorry to be using your only bag of supplies." I take the ice pack and place it on my ankle.

Pierce moves on his knees toward the front of the tent to see what the weather looks like. "No change, it's still raining cats and dogs out there. And no apology is necessary. I'm just glad I was out here to help." He smiles at me.

I nod in agreement, and I start to think about the obvious situation. The rain is not letting up and it's now around five in the evening. Even if the rain did magically stop, I would have no tent or bag and the hike back to my car, if it's even safe, is three hours—

without injury. We'll have to share this *one* tent. *All night.* My palms start to sweat with the idea. This is already breaking my comfort level. So, I do the one thing I know how: point out the obvious.

"So, Pierce, we're about to be really close for some time with this storm. How about we play a game?" I ask with a smile, hoping it hides my nervousness.

"Yeah, it seems this storm isn't going anywhere fast. So, what game?" he replies, returning the smile.

"I'll say two truths and a lie. You guess which is the lie?" I say, resting my chin on my knees.

"Okay, sounds fun," he responds, but I can see a small clench in his hand.

"I'll go first then. I am twenty-eight. I lived in Manhattan. I own a bakery," I say and then hide my smile.

He ponders the statements, bringing his fingers to his chin.

"You did not live in Manhattan," he says positively.

"Wrong," I say with a laugh.

"Really?! So, which was the lie?" he asks.

"That I own a bakery," I tell him. "Your turn."

"Wait, so if you don't bake amazing treats, what do you do?" he asks, throwing a hand to his chest for dramatic flare.

"I am actually a lawyer. Studied business and real estate mostly. And who said I can't bake amazing treats?" I reply, folding my arms across my chest to match his dramatics.

"Okay, okay," he says, putting his hands up in surrender and takes his turn. "I am thirty. I am a lawyer. I am divorced." He says each one slowly, evaluating my facial expressions to each.

I also take my time thinking about those statements. I look him over. His facial hair is at a five o'clock shadow stage, so he usually shaves. I look at his hands and do not see a ring on his finger or a tan line of one. He has a build that would look really nice in an Armani suit. He definitely works out. So maybe he's a lawyer—this guy does kind of remind me of Harvey Specter from *Suits*. The dim, battery-powered lantern casts a glow throughout the tent, allowing a glimpse of Pierce has sun-kissed, tan skin and short but wavy brown hair with golden streaks running through it. He has high cheekbones and eyes as dark as the midnight sky. I find myself getting lost in them when I realize I am just staring, so I break my gaze from him and say, "You are not divorced." I say it somewhat quietly, because I do not mean it as a judgment.

He laughs and shakes his head.

"Wrong. I am not a lawyer," he tells me.

"I meant no judgment; I was almost married. I left my fiancé three months ago." I'm not sure why I felt I should share that very personal information, but it's out there now.

"It's fine. Do you want to talk about it?"

I remove the ice pack to look at my ankle, noting that it already seems less swollen.

"Eh, the short version is he cheated. So I left him, and then I needed to leave Manhattan all together, so I quit my job at the firm and sold my townhome. I moved my stuff back in with my parents. I decided to live my life for me. So, I came out here to find solitude and peace. And hopefully a fresh perspective on my next move." I shrug my shoulders, not meeting his gaze.

"I'm so sorry, Leah. About your fiancé. Not about coming here or leaving Manhattan. I hate the city." He pauses for a moment, contemplating what he's going to say next. "I was married to my high school sweetheart. We both became financial advisors and started a firm in Sacramento. She cheated on me with one of our associates, so I had her buy me out of the firm, and we divorced. I left there and moved out here to a small town outside Moab, called Castle Valley, and started my own firm. That was about five years ago now. It's not Sacramento money, but it pays the bills, and I live comfortably. I, too, sought God in the matter." His eyes wander around the tent as he speaks, but this voice is strong, steady.

My heart hurts for him. But oddly enough, he knows what it's like to leave an entire life behind and start over. He understands my need for a fresh start better than anyone in this moment.

"I admire your courage to start over. How did you know what to do next?" I ask him.

"When I came out here to hike and sightsee for the first time, a random stranger that I had sparked a conversation with was saying how they needed a new financial advisor because the local guy had retired recently. It was the most random conversation, but I felt it was a sign." He shrugs.

"I get that. I wish my sign could be that obvious for me right now," I say with a small laugh.

I start to think about my situation and my desire to find direction. I can't recall the last time I traveled anywhere, besides a beach. That's sad. I frown a bit at my own thoughts. *God, can you tell me where I should go next?* I plead with him silently.

We played a few more rounds of the game and seemed to dry off a little thanks to the desert heat.

"So I take it you enjoy hiking?" Pierce asks.

"Yeah, I loved it. Sorry I ever stopped doing it," I reply.

Pierce quirks a brow at the statement, so I elaborate.

"My ex, he didn't like hiking or outdoors unless a beach or resort was involved. Also work became hectic. So I guess I stopped finding ways to pursue what I really loved to the fullest." I shrugged.

"Ah, I see. I mean, did the city have a lot of options for you, anyway?" he asks genuinely, not judgmentally.

"No, not for hiking, but they did hold a lot of

5k runs. I only did a Color Run once. And once in a while, I went to an indoor rock climbing gym while Grayson was at his gym."

He nodded in response.

"This storm is starting to ease up, but let's get some rest. I promise I will not murder you in your sleep."

"Oddly enough, I don't believe you would. Just don't kick me in the face," I say and laugh with him.

I lay with my head at one end of the tent, and he places his head at the other end next to my feet. Our backsides slightly press to one another due to the lack of space. Pierce gives me his sweater to use as a pillow, and we open his sleeping bag to create one large blanket for both of us. Before I fall asleep, I have to ask him one more question.

"Did you see me fall down the hill?"

"No, I heard a yell. By the time I came out of my tent, you were standing. I'm glad you missed the part where *I* slipped coming down after you," he says.

I chuckle a little because I can't help but imagine this man butt-sliding down the hill.

"You obviously aren't hurt, or I would not have laughed," I tell him.

"Nope, just my pride. Goodnight, Leah."

"Goodnight, Pierce. Thank you, again, for rescuing me."

I fall asleep to the sound of light rain tapping on the tent.

Chapter 5

PIERCE

THERE IS A WOMAN'S BACK pressed against mine in my *one-person* tent. If you had told me twelve hours ago this is where I would be, I would have laughed. But all joking aside, my heart aches for Leah and what she has been through. My heartbreak may have been five years ago, but there's still a part of me that knows exactly how she must be feeling. I also didn't want to embarrass her by telling her I did see her falling down the hill, so instead I told her *I slipped*, which gained a small laugh from her. She deserves to laugh.

I lay here with my eyes open, listening to the sound of the rain against the tent. Leah is brave for coming out here alone and hiking, but I understand why she did it. *I mean, I did the same thing.* I feel Leah take a deep, soothing breath, and her back seems to settle afterward, giving me the reassurance she is asleep.

When I knocked her out of the way of the boulder earlier, I didn't move off her right away because her bright blue eyes mesmerized me for a moment. Her dark hair was plastered against her face from the rain, but her vibrant ocean-blue eyes were like beacons. She has an olive skin tone that makes her eyes pop. I wonder if it's natural or from a tanning booth.

I squeeze my eyes tight, trying to quiet my thoughts so I can sleep. Finally, after about a half hour, the rain seems to slow, and I find myself drifting off when I'm randomly reminded of an old business idea: Grow the business so there's a legal side and a financial side. *She wanted a new beginning. What if I can offer her that?*

My mind is reeling, because on one hand, I know the Valley could use a good lawyer. The townspeople have been whispering about a few suits coming through. They're all worried about it becoming the next commercialized tourist attraction instead of the community it is. *Could Leah help?* What are the odds I end up caught in a storm with a lawyer who can possibly help Castle Valley?

My subconscious slides it into my thoughts: *Not to mention, she's pretty.*

I finally get my mind to settle and am able to somehow will myself to sleep.

Chapter 6

LEAH

THE RISE OF THE MORNING sun seeps through the tent, and I am careful not to rustle too much and wake Pierce, who is still sleeping. I'm a light sleeper, and the moment the sun comes up, my eyes usually open. I used to have blackout curtains in my townhouse so I could sleep late on my days off, but those became few and far between.

I pull out my phone and praise Jesus that the rain and multiple falls—one belly slide, one tackle—yesterday did not destroy it. The weather is going to be bright and sunny today with a high of 79 (I hope), and I see I have a missed call from my parents. I'm sure they were checking the weather and saw the storm. I send a text.

Me: Alive and well. hit a storm last night
but all is okay. I am hiking with a man
named Pierce, who I met on the trail.
Just want you to know in case I go
missing. Xo

No way am I telling them I am in a tent with a stranger. Cue freak out.

Mom: Okay thanks for the check in. Aim
true if need be. ;) be safe!

"Morning, Leah," I hear Pierce whisper.
I quickly place my phone down.
"Morning, Pierce," I whisper back. "I hope I didn't wake you," I say as I feel my cheeks flush a bit.
"No, I'm an early riser most days, so my internal clock wakes me."
We both sit up, and Pierce makes a move to unzip the tent and head outside.
"Leah, *come quick!*" Pierce shouts.
I stand in a hurry and rush out. And I stop immediately.
My eyes snap up to where Pierce stands facing the hill's edge, the same one we'd struggled to climb up during the storm. It takes me mere seconds to realize he's captivated by the large, faint rainbow that stretches across the horizon. I slowly walk toward him, as if

the rainbow would hear my footsteps and cease to exist if it caught me lurking.

"It's magnificent," I whisper, coming up beside Pierce.

"That it is," he whispers back.

Pierce doesn't speak again and neither do I. I find immediate comfort in the silent understanding between us that the rainbow should not be disturbed with sudden movement or loud voices. We both just admire the beauty of the land and moment before us.

It's nearly seven in the morning, so the sun is high enough that everything is cast in sunlight. You would never know that, a little over twelve hours ago, a storm ripped through here. The river below has receded back into its proper place. My tent is gone, nowhere to be seen.

I watch the rainbow fade slowly and ponder the irony of my life and this storm. My life flooded and washed away when I walked away from my fiancé and career, but after every storm comes a rainbow. God's promise doesn't call me to stay amid the wreckage. He calls me to a new day, and I will hold onto His promise and covenant. A few minutes later, the rainbow whisps away.

Pierce walks back toward the tent. I stay another moment in the quiet, gathering my newfound confidence and strength to face *my* new day.

And then I realize how bad I need a drink. I follow Pierce and ask.

"Do you have an extra bottle of water?"

"I have my Yeti in my bag, I only packed one. You can have some."

I uncap his Yeti and pour it into my mouth, trying my best not to touch the rim of his container. *Since I'm breaking all my comfort levels, what's one more?* After I have a sip of water, I help Pierce close up the tent and pack it away.

"Thank you again, Pierce. Are you headed out of the park?" I ask him.

"You're welcome. Yes, I am, gotta head back home. Tomorrow is a workday, for me, that is." He smirks.

"Yeah, I remember those days," I reply coyly.

Pierce laughs. I have no supplies, and I desperately need a shower. So, I guess I'm heading out of the park, too.

"I will walk out with you, if that's okay?" I ask him.

"I would love the company," Pierce says happily.

On the hike back, Pierce helps me navigate some rough spots where the rain must have shifted some of the rocks, and he asks every now and then how my ankle is holding up. *He is such a gentleman.* He stops me about fifteen miles later.

"Oh, here!" he exclaims, waving at me to follow him off the path. "Let me show a spot I'm sure you didn't know about."

"Ah, *this* is the part where you kill me!" I yell out, laughing but following him.

We go a quarter mile off the path, and I see an opening in the mountain. Pierce takes out his flashlight from his pack. When we are standing at the entrance to the cave, he turns on the flashlight and looks back at me.

"You ready to be blown away?" He grins.

I smile and nod back at him with pure anticipation for what he's about to show me. Pierce slowly lifts the flashlight, which begins to illuminate the black space. Almost instantly, I see the sparkle against the light as giant crystals hang from all around the cavern. Most of them are a beautiful white, but some have streaks of pure ocean blue running through them.

"Oh my goodness! This is just . . ." I can't even finish my sentence.

"I know," is all he says.

"Why are some of them blue?" I ask as I walk into the cave to touch some of the crystal that runs up the walls.

"When there's no oxygen running though the water, it creates a natural blue color."

"How did you find this place?" I ask.

"I stumbled upon it one day when I needed to . . . uhm . . ." He pauses and his cheeks redden.

"Oh." I laugh so hard my belly hurts. "I'm sorry, I'm sorry. It's just, you found one of the most beautiful spots I have ever seen all because you needed a pee break."

Pierce begins to laugh right alongside me.

"When you gotta go, you gotta go," he says, shrugging his shoulders.

I take out my phone to snap a picture of the cavern. We continue hiking out of the park and admire a few other sights along the way. Pierce and I laugh and joke the entire way. We even take a selfie at one of the arches.

"My arm isn't long enough to capture both of us with your height!" I tell him, laughing while trying to hold out my phone.

"Here." He takes my phone from me and snaps the photo.

"So, you said you practiced real estate law, right?" he asks, changing the subject a bit abruptly.

"I did, mostly for big corporations, though. Why do you ask?" I look over to him.

"The town I'm in. It's a very close community and there have been whispers of suits coming in possibly looking to—"

"Commercialize it," I say, pointedly interrupting him.

"I assume so," he replies.

"Oh, they are. They did it to my hometown in Jersey. There is some weird air law that the town could look into with a local lawyer to try and keep them away. After watching my town turn into a tourist attraction, it drove me to want to understand it all.

Guess it's what drove me into law in the first place." I give some more advice and we continue walking.

Honestly, Pierce feels like a friend I've known forever. I'm so comfortable around him. I'm thankful our paths crossed even if it has been for this short amount of time.

We reach the lot where we left our cars. Thankfully, the flash flood did not do any damage here. He walks me over to my car, and I almost wish we weren't parting ways.

Chapter 7

PIERCE

WE EXIT THE PARK, AND I walk her over to her car. The hike out was the most fun I have had with a woman in a long time. We just seemed to click. My thoughts resurface about asking her to help in town and possibly roll in legal with my firm. But more so about saving Castle Valley from poachers now that I know she knows so much about the process. *I could ask her to come back to town and check it out. Would that be weird? The worst she could say is no.*

"Will you head back to New Jersey?" I ask her.

"Probably. I lost most of my supplies so three days will have to be enough. For now, anyway."

"What about work?" I ask her, running my hand through my hair and to the back of my neck.

"I don't know. I loved being a lawyer, but I signed a non-compete, so I can't work for two years within one hundred miles of my old job. I'll figure it out, though." She replies with a shrug.

"You know, if you ever wanted to start over somewhere, not in the city, I could use you at my firm. We could have a finance side and a legal side. I had thought about that a time or two but never had the right candidate for it. Someone I could trust. But more than that, I'm wondering if you could maybe help me save Castle Valley? I hope I'm not overstepping. Just felt prompted to say it." I stammer all of this out, trying not to ramble, but that was inevitable.

"And how would you know I'm the right candidate? That you could trust me?" she asks, staring directly into my eyes.

I meet her gaze and don't look away. "Because I don't believe in coincidence." I tell her confidently. "What if this is God's way of answering both of our prayers?"

Leah is quiet for what feels like minutes, so to break the tension, I add: "Think on it. Let me get my business card from my car for you."

I turn from her and stride three cars over to mine.

Chapter 8

LEAH

I BEGIN TO THINK ABOUT how I'd asked God for help. And then Pierce had showed up. And I had prayed last night about giving me direction. What if this is it? What if, right here, is where I start a new adventure, a new chapter of my life?

But with a guy? Do I really want to do that?

What's the harm in looking around, even if I don't stay for the job? I could maybe, at least, point the town in a good direction to help them. I could just book a flight for tomorrow instead of heading to the airport now. I contemplate for a moment.

"Pierce!" I shout his name.

He pops his head over the top of his car, and because I'm standing at my trunk, I can see him.

"I am willing to hear you out and have you show me around. My flight isn't until tomorrow morning."

I see his smile widen, and I return it with pure excitement.

"I know a great bed-and-breakfast where you could stay for the night in town. I'd love to show you around. Follow me to Castle Valley?" he asks.

I nod and get into my car.

An hour later, we pull up outside the Castle Valley B&B. It's a quaint little place shaped like a castle. Its aura gives off historical vibes on the outside. But on the inside, it's completely modernized from colors to furniture. I love it. It's unique.

"There was an older woman who owned it for years, but when she passed away, her daughter took it over and redecorated. But she wanted to make sure the outside stayed true to its historical nature," Pierce tells me, almost as if he's read my mind.

"Well, she did great job," I reply, still taking in the views of the sitting room by the front desk.

"Pierce, good to see you. What brings you in?" a slender middle-aged woman calls out.

"Hi, Susan, I need a room for a night for my friend here. Leah, this is Susan. Susan, Leah." He motions toward me, and I step up and extend my hand to shake Susan's.

"Welcome to Castle Valley, Leah! You have already met one of our finest. Let me get you a room." She shakes my hand and smiles before she rummages through her scheduling book.

Once I'm checked in, I tell Pierce I'd like to freshen up after the night we had, and he understands.

"It's just about two o'clock. How about I come back around five. We can go to dinner, and I'll show you around?" he asks.

"That's perfect. See you in a bit." I give him an awkward little wave and then head toward the stairs.

As I near the door to my room, I halt, remembering that I have no clothes except hiking attire. *I can't wear yoga pants and an athletic shirt to dinner.*

I head back to the front desk where the woman who had helped me seems to have gone away.

"Excuse me?" I say, somewhat loud, hoping anybody will answer.

"Sorry, be right there!" she replies back.

I patiently wait for her return and walk over to the decorative electric fireplace in the wall by the sitting area. It isn't giving off any heat but shimmers different colors.

"How can I help you?" she asks from behind me.

"Sorry to bother you, but I realized my clothes all got ruined and I'll need to go get some before I can shower and change. Could you recommend a nearby store?"

"Of course! On the main road is a small shop called Ellie-Mae's, she should have a good selection."

"Perfect. Thank you."

"No problem at all. Please let me know if you need anything else," she says with a smile and goes back to the front desk.

After about a ten-minute walk up the main road, I locate Ellie-Mae's Boutique. The shop is very well lit inside, illuminating all the wonderfully thrifty clothing pieces. *My town used to have the best thrift clothing store.* I can feel my pulse quicken with excitement about this store. When I walk in, a young woman immediately greets me.

"Welcome to Ellie-Mae's. Oh, you're a new face 'round here. I am the owner, Ellimina Mae. You can call me Ellie, of course." Her Southern accent, paired with the creativity of the shop, makes me feel so welcomed, I can't help but smile.

"Hi, yes, pleasure to meet you, Ellie, you have a beautiful store. I am only in town for the night, but I have dinner plans. It was unexpected and I only brought hiking attire. My name is Leah."

"Well, you're in the right place. Let's see what we find ya." Ellie motions for me to follow her.

Yes, lead me into a shopping spree. Take all my money for this feeling right here.

A hot shower, one yellow sundress, and some sandals later, and I feel like a brand-new woman. I blow-dried my long, chestnut hair and even did my makeup. I look down at my phone and see it's just before five o'clock. *Perfect.* I also see the confirmation for the flight I booked before I went in the shower.

I walk down the stairs and hear Pierce talking with Susan at the front desk. They aren't speaking loud enough to make out their conversation, but the closer I get to the front, the easier it is to see Susan has a smile on her face and Pierce is leaning against the desk. Pierce is wearing khaki shorts with a navy-blue polo and Hey Dude shoes. Susan sees me coming and alerts Pierce, who stands, his eyes gliding over me. Butterflies begin to flutter in my stomach at his gaze. As his eyes meet mine, he smiles brightly and waits for me by the desk.

"Don't you clean up nice," he says playfully.

"What? Mud and rain didn't suit me? You're not so bad yourself," I play back.

"See you later, Susan. Let me know if you need an appointment," he tells her with a small wave as he makes his way toward the front door.

So, he was talking about work with her. I follow him to the front door, which he holds open for me. Susan waves at us, and I don't hesitate to smile and wave back.

"After you." He tips his head down.

"Thank you. So, where are we headed?" I ask him.

When he comes through the door, he stands beside me and motions to the right.

"We are going to an Italian restaurant in the center of town. But I hope you don't mind walking. It's better to see the main strip and the town this way."

"I don't mind walking. Although I did have to take a run to Ellie-Mae's earlier so I may have spoiled seeing some of the town." I smile at him, twisting my hands.

"Ah, so you met Ellie already then?" he asks.

"Yes, she was charming, and I just *loved* her store. I had to talk myself out of not buying everything, but I did grab this dress and a few suit dresses, too." I bit my inner cheek while smirking. "It reminded me of a store I used to love back home. Before the bigwigs moved in."

Pierce nods and gives me a sad smile. I can see that he's scared for his town. I hope I can help him somehow.

Chapter 9

PIERCE

WE WALK THE MAIN STRIP, and I tell her all about the different shops we pass and how most of them are all small businesses and family owned. She has already met Ellie at the boutique, and Susan with the B&B. She pauses in front of a printing press shop, so I gently take her hand and walk her inside. Leah's eyes light up with amazement at the actual ink press inside.

"Do you guys still print papers here?" she asks.

"We sure do! Only small-scale local things, but it gives some nostalgia to us old folks," Fred, the owner of the shop, says with a wink.

He is clearly amused and happy to have someone new to talk to, and in response to Leah's eagerness, he offers to give her an entire walkthrough of the press.

After the tour, we continue walking through town, making our way toward the restaurant. Leah was like a kid in a candy store admiring all the stores and greeting all the people alongside me like she has been here and known them forever.

"There's not much commercial business out here, as you can tell," I tell her. "Not many chains. You have to drive a little bit to get to the big box stores."

"That's nice, though. Makes the community actually feel like a community. I miss this feeling, especially after so many years in New York," Leah inputs with a smile.

Watching her take in the town causes my stomach to flutter a bit. Leah is a very attractive woman. Even last night in the rain I could tell. But now that she's in this yellow dress and all done up, it's even more prominent. I divert my gaze just before I make a fool of myself and miss the restaurant.

"Here we are." I reach for the door and hold it open for her.

Leah seems to hesitate for a moment before going in. I noticed this earlier at the B&B, too, almost like she isn't used to someone opening doors for her.

She casts her head down and heads inside. "Thank you," she says quietly as she walks by.

"This is the best fried calamari I have ever tasted," Leah says as she pops another piece into her mouth and closes her eyes, savoring it.

"Told you. Are you a foodie?" I ask her.

"Yes! I love great food. All kinds. You?" she asks me, wiping the corner of her mouth with the napkin.

"I like to try new things often, but I also am a guy who likes my favorites." I reach for my beer and take a sip.

"Do you drink often?" she asks after I put my glass back down.

"No, one beer occasionally here and there."

"Same, but wine or sangria, not beer."

The waiter comes over and brings our entrees. Leah got the spaghetti and meatballs while I got the salmon francaise over linguini. We make small talk throughout our dinner, but the food keeps most of our concentration.

"So where are you from before the city?" I ask her.

"A small town in New Jersey called Roan. It was a lot like Castle Valley until . . . well, you know," she replied between a forkful of pasta. "How about you before Sacramento?"

"I actually was born and raised just outside there, so I was used to commercialized areas. Castle Valley was a change for me. A good one, though."

A little while later, the waiter, Tom, stops by. "Can I clear your plates and offer you any dessert, coffee, or tea?"

"I am finished, thank you," Leah says.

I nod at Tom to take my dish as well, giving him my thanks. "I'm going to have a coffee, please. Leah, would you like anything else?"

"Oh, I'd like some coffee, too." She smiles and Tom vanishes with our plates and coffee order.

"So, what do you think of Castle Valley so far?" I ask her.

"I think it is a really sweet, homey town. I love that everyone is so close-knit. I'm sorry I keep bringing it up, but I grew up in a town like this and, honestly, I forgot what it felt like. Manhattan, as I'm sure you can imagine from its similarities to Sacramento, is all hustle and bustle, no quietness." I can hear the longing in her tone.

"I remember that about Sacramento, yes."

Words are on the tip of my tongue, words that I could string together that would suggest she stay here, where it's quiet, where it's homey, where hiking and adventure is just a short drive away. I can offer her a new community to replace the one she lost and misses, and I can offer her a means to afford it all. But second guessing gets the better of me and I don't say any of those words. Because I'm not sure we should work together. *I might like her too much.*

Chapter 10

LEAH

DINNER WAS AMAZING. THE FOOD was some of the best Italian I have had in a long time. It was unexpected for such a small town.

Pierce and I are strolling at a leisurely place through the downtown toward a local creamery where they make homemade gelato and ice cream.

"I love ice cream. It's my kryptonite," I tell him while laughing.

"Good to know. What's your favorite flavor?"

"Mint chocolate chip, for sure, but I also love a really good chocolate vanilla swirl in a cone with rainbow sprinkles. You?"

"That was oddly specific." He pauses, and I can tell by the crinkle of his eyes and the smile that plays on his lips that he's amused by me. I like it. "I like coffee flavor the best."

We enter the creamery, and the intoxicating scent of sweet cream immediately consumes me. My mouth waters at the thought of how good this will be.

"They make everything themselves except the toppings. If I can't convince you to stay, maybe this place will."

I can feel my cheeks flush lightly at his admission of wanting me to stay. I don't want to dwell on that thought, so I playfully exclaim: "They don't make the toppings? I can't eat here now." I fold my arms and stick my nose up as I walk past him and toward the counter.

Pierce's laugh filters behind me. We stay true to our favorite flavors and take a seat by the window. Pierce refused to let me pay for dessert even though he had paid for dinner, too.

"Is there a reason you're not off the market?" I don't meet his eyes after I ask the question.

I probably shouldn't have asked.

"I'm sorry. You know what? That was not appropriate. We barely know each other. Forget I asked. It's none of my business." I take another spoonful of my ice cream to prevent anything else absurd coming out of my mouth.

"No, it's okay, really, Leah. I am single simply because I haven't met someone who is true to who they are in person and on social media or online profiles and who seemed to click well with me. You know, the feeling of just simply having a good time without really trying so hard."

I lift my eyes and realize Pierce is staring right at me. My nerves begin to tingle at his gaze. I think about his answer, and I do know what he means. *It's how I feel right now.* Simply being with one another, enjoying the company, and not hiding or pretending.

With his right hand, Pierce brings a napkin to the corner of my mouth and dabs away the mint ice cream that must have dripped in my hurry to shut my mouth. I watch as if time has painfully slowed. It was such a simple, careful, but confident gesture that most men wouldn't have performed. In fact, my first date with Grayson, I had smudged gravy on my cheek somehow and he didn't bother to tell me—our waiter had told me when he came to clear our plates. *That was so embarrassing.* Pierce's hand slowly pulls away, and I can immediately feel the sense of yearning for his hand to touch me again.

"Thank you," I tell him with a small smile.

Pierce is silent but returns the smile. *I wonder what he's thinking right now.*

"It's getting late. We should head back to the B&B," Pierce announces, checking his watch.

It's just after eight in the evening. And I do have a seven o'clock flight, which means five o'clock airport arrival. I nod in agreement, clean up our cups, and follow him out the door. The walk back is nearly silent, but I can sense his eyes glancing over at me every so often. When we reach the front door of the B&B, we face each other under the awning of the drop-off area.

"Thank you for showing me around town, Pierce, and for saving my life in the park." I extend my hand to shake his.

"My pleasure for both," he replies, taking my hand and shaking it, but he doesn't let go right away.

A moment passes and the butterflies in my stomach begin again. I look down to our clasped hands and then back up to Pierce. Just as I am about to say something, he releases my hand and runs his through his dark hair, ruffling the otherwise gelled-back perfection. It suddenly hits me.

"We never talked about your offer," I state.

Pierce smirks before he replies, and my heart does a mini summersault at that slow grin.

"No, we didn't. I enjoyed your company more than talking work, it seems. If you have any suggestions for how I can help protect this town, or any solid leads, you have my business card. Please email me or call. Thank you for a wonderful couple of days, Leah."

My heart fractures a bit at his words. *Maybe he thinks I'm not a good fit after all.* I have a hard time finding words because I am conflicted. When I finally find my voice, I tell him, simply, "Goodnight, Pierce."

As I open the front door to the B&B, which feels like dead weight, I take one final glance over my shoulder and see Pierce wave before turning and walking off.

I should be asleep, it's nearly midnight, but there are a million thoughts running through my head preventing sleep. I pick up my phone and send a text to Chelsea.

Me: Hey you awake?

I instantly see the bubbles appear that indicate she's typing.

Chelsea: Yea, everything okay?

I don't bother responding with a text. I just press the Call button and place the phone to my ear.

"Hey, what's wrong?" Chelsea's voice has a worried tone to it.

"Nothing, everything is fine actually. I just need to talk this all out."

"Okay, shoot." I can hear the ruffling of her covers as she gets ready for whatever is about to be said.

I tell her everything. From the hike, to the storm,

I tell her about Pierce saving my life and how I spent a night in his tent. I tell her about how he showed me around town and the feelings I'm developing toward him. Chelsea listens and adds the occasional "uh-huh" to let me know she's still with me.

"This town is just so quaint, and I really love its vibe. I could see myself starting fresh out here on my own. The town does need some legal help, which I know I can do. But I don't want Pierce to think I am only staying because of him, because that would be lame." I finish with a long exhale because I think, throughout the entire story, I didn't bother with one.

"Leah, we have been best friends since kindergarten. Our entire lives, you never, and I mean *never* followed others, not even a guy. With Grayson . . . well . . . I think you got comfortable with the idea of being safe, checking off boxes, and just doing what was expected, what came next in life. I think you have always had this idea about how you thought life would go and it kind of blew up for you. The Leah I knew loved hiking and adventuring. Remember our trip to the Smokies?" she asks and pauses.

"Yeah, that was the last time I was outdoors like that," I tell her sheepishly, not wanting to admit that since it was almost seven years ago.

"You glowed out there in those mountains. I told you then that I swore you would live in the mountains one day. That was seven years ago, Leah. *Seven.* You need to live your life how you *want* to. Not how you think you have to or are supposed to." She is speaking *into* me. "If you want to stay in this town because you like it, stay. Try it. As far as this thing with Pierce, you could take it slow and tell him why you decided to stay. Make it about the town, about the opportunities to help the people, about you—not about him—but let him know he could be a part of your future."

"He had wanted to talk business but never did. What if he doesn't want me to stay after spending time with me? I don't want to make things awkward."

"I think any guy would be crazy not to like you. I think he is a smart man who understands what it's like to start over and come from hurt. Maybe he just is giving you the chance to decide without his pressure," she replies confidently.

"I hadn't thought of it that way," I admit while I play with the edge of the quilt on the bed.

"I got you. No matter what you want." She changes the subject. "What time is your flight tomorrow?"

"Seven."

"Okay, I'll see you when you're back. Get some rest."

I throw myself back against the pillow with a sigh, the rush of a story having led me to sit up to deliver it in all its glory. "Night, Chels," I say, and we hang up.

I do love the mountains and hiking. Moving here puts me well out of my non-compete territory and gives me an abundance of national parks to visit quite often. I don't think I could ever tire of the beautiful views. I do have a small attraction to Pierce, but it can't be the reason I stay.

God, what should I do?

Chapter 11

PIERCE

THE MOMENT I LIFTED THAT napkin to wipe the ice cream off the corner of her mouth, I knew I was in trouble. I knew there was no way I could talk with her about business, because I would have been selfish in my pursuit. I want her to stay, but not for business. Although this town could use a good lawyer, I can't ask that of her, not after what she just went through.

The way Leah's eyes had watched me but didn't stop me lets me know, at least a little bit, that she must feel this attraction, too.

Or she was stunned by my actions and didn't know what to do.

I drag my hand over my face as I stare at myself in the mirror of my bathroom. I have to let her go. The truth is that even if she did miraculously decide to stay for any reason, I wouldn't be able to mesh her into the business. I think we have both learned from the burns we endured. We would need to keep it separate. *Oh, who am I kidding, she isn't staying.*

I had a true connection with a woman for the first time in years, and I will have to let her leave. I click off the light as I leave the bathroom and slam myself onto my bed.

Sleep doesn't come, not at all.

I am staring at the ceiling when my alarm goes off. I take a deep breath and get out of bed. I grab my suit for the day, get dressed, and walk to the local coffee shop.

Betty greets me over the crowded room. "Morning, Pierce. The usual?"

"You know me well, Betty." I smile at her and leave her a five-dollar tip in the jar.

"You are always too good to me. Heard you had a girl out on the town last night?" She quirks a brow at me in question.

Only thing bad about a small town: *Everyone knows everything.*

"Yes, just a friend I was showing around. She went back home this morning," I tell her as I grab my coffee.

"Shame, you deserve happiness. And from the gossip, you two were quite smitten. . . . Have a good day," she tells me before turning to help the next customer.

Smitten *I* was.

I leave the coffee shop and greet the other shop owners as they're opening their doors for the day. When I get to my office front, I notice the lights on inside. *Odd.* I slowly reach for the door handle with my keys in hand and realize it's already open, too. I slowly open the door and take a step inside.

"Jane?" I call out over the space.

I hear footsteps quickly coming from the back toward me. The slight scuffle tells me they're Jane's. She's an older woman who needed a small job after retiring last year. I didn't really need any admin help, but it was something for her to do.

"Mr. Brighton, good morning. I was early today. And good thing, too. A client was waiting for you."

A client? I look down at my watch while simultaneously telling her, "Good morning. Jane, but it's only eight thirty. I don't usually book anyone until nine. It must be Mr. Jacobs. No worries. Thank you."

I head right to my office, not giving Jane a chance to confirm or correct me.

Mr. Jacobs is the hardware store owner, and I know he has been having financial strains lately. I had him scheduled for nine this morning, but he must be worried about something. It's okay—I would be, too, if I might lose my business a year before retirement.

"Mr. Jacobs, I am sorry to keep you—" I halt in the doorway, eyes nearly popping out of my head.

"Pierce Brighton. Brighton Financial. Has a nice ring to it." Her voice glides over the space and hits me right in the chest.

"L-Leah?" I question, dropping my briefcase beside the door. "You're here?" I must still be asleep. There is no way.

"Before you freak out or anything," she starts and puts her hands up like she's surrendering. "I decided to stay because of how much I loved this town and its vibes. I just want to make that clear." She keeps her eyes locked on mine.

I can't help the slight let-down that must flick across my face, but I steel that quickly. I swallow, unsure how to reply.

Oh, I'm glad you wanted to stay, but I kind of like you and you obviously don't want anything to do with me.

Leah gracefully walks over to me and stands five feet in front of me. My eyes wander and determine she looks very nice in her dress suit, but I snap them back up to her face at the next word.

"But . . ." she adds, slowly bringing her gaze to mine. "You are a nice bonus that comes with it. . . . Maybe," she speaks softly and fumbles with her hands at the remark, casting her eyes to the ground.

I smile the widest I think I ever have. My cheeks are instantly burning. I finally find the words to speak. I reach for one of her hands and hold it tenderly in mine.

"I would like that. I'd like to see where this goes with us. But I understand if you need to take it slow. I also think we shouldn't merge businesses, at least not right away, if we may have feelings for each other." I lose my smile at the last sentence hoping she understands.

"I couldn't agree more. I understand the hesitancy to merge. We have both been hurt and worked alongside those people. We can just take it slow across the board." She smiles at me, and I know that smile is something I will never tire of.

Epilogue

LEAH

One Year Later

"I WILL NEVER BE ABLE to thank you enough for saving my business, Ms. Peterson," Betty replies, hugging me tight.

I give her a squeeze in response. "It was my pleasure, Betty. No need for the formality. You know you can call me Leah."

Making Castle Valley permanent has proven to be a wise decision. About three months after I settled into my new office space, investment realtors started coming around and harassing local business owners to sell. Apparently, they sent spies out first to gauge the area, which was what all the gossip and concern had been about when I'd first met Pierce. As suspected, most land and business owners did not want to sell. But that did not stop the men in fancy suits and briefcases from coming. My previous research into the smart air space law came in handy, and I used it to guarantee the local businesses would be safe for good. Today was the final hearing.

"Dinner on me one night, Leah. No buts," Betty sternly tells me.

"I look forward to it," I reply with a wave good-bye.

A few other townsfolk also thank me as they pass by on their way out of the courthouse. I turn from the stairs of the courthouse and look out over the small town and smile. I just saved this town from going the way of my hometown. And that feels better than great. I became a lawyer to do good for the people, and for the first time in my whole career, it finally feels that way.

My cell ringing in my pocket distracts me from my moment, and I reach into my purse to retrieve it.

"Hello."

"Hello, beautiful, how was court?" Pierce asks.

"It worked! We won. No investment realtors will be seeking space in Castle Valley again anytime soon!" I exclaim with a small squeal.

"That is *great*. Worthy of celebrating over dinner tonight at the Italian place. Say seven o'clock?" Pierce says, overjoyed.

"I'll see you then! Bye." I smile and hang up and start walking back to my apartment.

When I had decided to stay and showed up at his office last year, we'd agreed to take things slow. We went out to dinner a few times and he, as well as others from the town, were very helpful in helping me move my stuff into the apartment I rented. About three months after I moved everything, Pierce and I made things official and became a couple. Our connection was real and genuine. That same week, my parents and Chelsea had come out to visit and I made it the best opportunity for them to meet Pierce, who I had spoken so fondly of.

Pierce, being the gentleman he is, shook both my parents' hands during introductions. "It is a pleasure to meet you both. You've raised a wonderful daughter," he'd said.

It had made me blush, and it still does when I think about it.

Long story short, they both adored him. My mother even encouraged us to move faster. I had given her a stern look to back off that topic, which she understood. I didn't need her to scare him off. The night my parents left was the night Pierce and I had our first kiss.

"Your mom is a sweet woman. She loves you," he'd said as he came up to embrace me from behind while I was wiping down the kitchen counter.

I had placed the rag down and turned to face him, pressing my back against the counter and lacing my arms around his neck.

"She does, but don't let her scare you with her comments." I'd felt I needed to say that to him.

"Oh, don't worry, I don't scare off easily," he'd replied, tucking away a stray hair that had fallen in my face.

The contact of his hand against my cheek made me relax into him, and instead of pulling his hand away, he'd cupped the back of my head, bringing his forehead to mine. A long moment passed. Then he whispered:

"I am going to kiss you now, Leah."

"Please do," I whispered back.

He'd gently moved his lips to mine in what started as a sweet kiss but soon turned into an all-consuming, can't-get-close-enough kiss. My fingers had laced in his hair while his one hand tangled in mine and he placed the other on my waist, locking me in his space. When Pierce finally pulled away, I couldn't open my eyes. I was afraid I had dreamt of the most perfect kiss and I would wake up and he wouldn't be there. To my gain, when my eyes relented, Pierce had been right there holding onto me. Real. I knew prior to that kiss, but there was no denying it after, not even a little—I was falling in love with him.

Pierce and I have kept our businesses separate, but we talk about our days with each other and sometimes lean on one another if we need advice. We take weekends and go hiking as often as the weather allows. We just booked a trip to Yellowstone, too.

I make it back to my apartment with an hour to spare. *Perfect.* I take a quick shower to fix my hair and makeup, and I change into something cute for dinner. I go with an auburn maxi dress and white cardigan. I also grab a pair of wedges to match. I am out the door and walking to the restaurant with just enough time.

Pierce is outside waiting for me when I walk up.

"Hi, handsome." I greet him with a small kiss on his lips.

For once, I don't need to go on my tiptoes since my wedges gave me some height.

"Hi. You look beautiful," he tells me, taking my hand in his as he opens the door to the restaurant.

This is the same restaurant where, one year ago, we had dinner after he saved me from being crushed by a boulder and nearly drowning in a flash flood. I have no doubt that this is why he chose this place tonight. The hostess smiles at us, but Pierce leads me past her to a table in the corner.

"Pierce, uh . . ." I try to ask him why he is choosing his own table, but my words fall off at the sight before me.

In the corner of the room is a candlelit table with a bottle of champagne sitting chilled in an ice bucket. A lovely small bouquet of red roses sits upon the center of the table. Directly behind the table are light-up letters with the phrase *Marry me?*

I stand there, awestruck, but can feel the tears welling up beneath my eyelids. I can't feel Pierce's hand holding mine anymore. *Because it isn't.* I turn toward him and see him down on one knee. My hands immediately come up to cover my mouth as I look into his eyes. I can feel myself slightly shaking.

"Leah Peterson, I knew the moment I wiped ice cream off your face a year ago that my heart wanted to belong to you. This last year has been nothing short of amazing with you. Our connection is as genuine as they come. You are the one I want to spend the rest of my life hiking through mountains and life with. Will you marry me?" He spoke the words without a hint of nervousness but with pure confidence.

I can feel the tears slowly streaking down my face. I stare at this perfect man before me, and I know I feel the same. When I came to Utah, my heart was broken. I felt lost. I found myself again in those arches. I found my purpose in this town. And I knew months ago I had found my person. I have never felt more sure that I am right where I should be than I do in this very moment.

"Pierce Brighton, yes," I replied, my heart racing.

Pierce took my left hand into his and slipped on a magnificent opal-shaped diamond set in a gold band on my ring finger. I hadn't even bothered to look at the ring box he was holding open. It didn't matter if it was a rubber band, I still would have said yes. He stood up and wrapped his arms around me as I wrapped mine around his neck. He pulled me in close and lifted me off the ground. It was a picture-perfect moment.

As we sat and had dinner, we drank champagne and toasted to ourselves. While Pierce ordered us dessert and coffee, I looked down at the ring, lost in thoughts of the last year. I am happy all because of change.

Change can be hard. Accepting change in my life was hard. But change is the only thing that can keep us moving forward. Change breaks barriers of comfort we place upon ourselves for safety. Change is the thing that needs to happen to unlock the potential we didn't know was possible. God has a purpose for all our roads in life. He knows our steps. He promises He will work all things for our good. And today I am grateful for the storm I faced in order to get to higher ground.

THE END

AUTHOR'S NOTE

Thank you for reading *The Hike to Higher Ground!* I hope you enjoyed the story as much as I enjoyed bringing it to life. This story holds a special place in my heart because it has some very personal attributes woven into its pages.

I have had a love in my life that suppressed me and what I loved without even realizing it. Having to walk away was hard. The change that came and the chapter that unfolded has brought me to the wonderful life I live now. I met my real life "Pierce," and I pray someday, if you haven't already, you find yours. Everyone is worthy of a love that transforms them into the best versions of themselves.

Grateful to you, my readers, always. Please find me on Instagram to follow along for more exciting stories in the future. I kindly ask that you leave a review on your preferred review site if you can. Thank you and happy reading!

ACKNOWLEDGMENTS

I want to first and formally thank God for blessing me with this gift. I now know that all roads have led me right here. Hence my dedication.

Secondly, I want to thank my husband, Chris, who has supported me through discovering this new ability and encouraged me to pursue it. Chris, thank you for showing me a love that perseveres and conquers challenges.

Thirdly, I thank my sister in Christ and best friend, Kim, for endlessly listening to me about this chapter in my life and also being one of the main encouragers, BETA readers, and supporters in this process. Thank you for being a rock in my life. I am thankful every day God ordained this friendship.

Lastly, I would not be able to have done this without my family and other very close friends who also read and encouraged my new dream.

All in all, none of this would have been possible without any of the aforementioned people's encouragement and positive words. A simple thank-you will never be enough.

I also want to acknowledge my daughter, Ellery, for reminding me to always have faith, like a child, in our Lord. It is through her "blind" obedience (but sometimes defiance) that I can understand how great our God is to me every day. His patience, gentleness, and love amaze me. My prayer for you, my daughter, is that you always follow God and chase what he puts on your heart.

Finally, a thank-you to Nicole Frail, my publisher, for taking the chance on me. You have been nothing short of patient, understanding, encouraging, and kind. Thank you from the bottom of my heart for all you have done to help make this possible!

ABOUT THE AUTHOR

ALYSSA FELICIANO is a mother, wife, homemaker, and follower of Jesus Christ. Alyssa found her passion for books after becoming a mother. She then discovered her love of writing about two years later. Alyssa's original degree was in Surgical Technology and Applied Science. She worked in Labor and Delivery for most of her career but retired that career in 2022 when she felt God calling her to stay home with her newborn. Through following God's will, Ayssa has been able to activate and press into her writing abilities. Alyssa writes stories that channel love and hope in both contemporary and fantasy settings, finding ways to honor God within her writing as often as possible. She truly enjoys sharing her creativity with the world and hopes it will change hearts and minds in the process. Her ultimate goal is to provide young adults wholesome stories to read.

She is also the author of *Love's Flame: A Romantasy Short Story*, which won the Christlit Book Award in 2025.

Find Alyssa on Instagram at:
@alyssafwrites

ALSO AVAILABLE

LOVE'S FLAME

Winner of the Christlit Book Award 2025!

Love, like a fire, can burn you, or ignite you. Sometimes, it's both.

1 Corinthians 13; 4-7 tells us: "Love is patient, love is kind. It does not envy. It is not self-seeking, and it not easily angered. It always protects, always trusts, always hopes, always perseveres."

Fenix is a high-born fae who will one day rule over Ellewood as its High Lord. In the interim, a war looms beyond their realm. Fenix's powers are unmatched. He is the key to defeating the Dark One. Coraline knew better than to fall in love with him, that one day her status as a lesser fae would tear them apart. On the night before Fenix leaves for battle, Cora makes a decision that alters everything.

Available as an e-book.

Attic Books and Attic Ebooks
are imprints of Nicole Frail Books, LLC,
an independent ("indie") publishing
company located in Avoca, Pennsylvania.

Attic Ebooks is a digital-first imprint and is
open to submissions of various lengths,
including short stories and essays and
novellas. If the length and market allows,
longer works are considered for print with
Attic Books.

To learn more about submitting a query to
Attic Ebooks, visit www.attic-ebooks.com.

Readers!
Join the NFB Street Team for exclusive first
reads and swag from Attic & Attic Ebooks!
www.nicolefrailbooks.com/street